WALT DISNEY PRODUCTIONS

presents

101 DALMATIANS

Random House New York

Library of Congress Cataloging in Publication Data
Disney (Walt) Productions. Walt Disney's 101 Dalmatians. (Disney's wonderful world of reading, #23) Two dalmatians
rescue their own ten puppies plus eighty-nine more held captive by dog thieves. [1. Dogs—Fiction] I. Title. II. Title:
101 Dalmatians. PZ7.D6250p6 [E] 74-10829 ISBN 0-394-82571-3 ISBN 0-394-92571-8 (lib. bdg.)
Manufactured in the United States of America

1 2 3 4 5 6 7 8 9 0

C D E F G H I J K
6 7 8

Once there were ten Dalmatian puppies.
Pongo was their father.
Perdy was their mother.
They all lived in a house in the city
with two very nice people.

One day the puppies went for a walk.

A woman named Cruella was going by
in her car.

Cruella was a dog thief!

As soon as she saw the puppies,
she stopped to count them.

"TEN!" she cried. "Ten Dalmatian
puppies! I must have them."

Two men worked for Cruella.

Their names were Horace and Jasper.

Horace was short, fat, and dumb.

Jasper was tall, thin, and dumb.

"I want those puppies," she told them.

"Get them—TONIGHT!"

That night Jasper and Horace sneaked
into the house where the Dalmatians lived.
Everyone was asleep.
They put the puppies in a big, black bag.
Then they climbed out the window.
The puppies began to bark inside the bag.

Pongo and Perdy woke up.
The basket was empty!
The puppies were gone!

"Where are the puppies?" cried Perdy.
"I don't know," said Pongo.

Then Pongo had an idea.
"We will send a message to all the dogs
in the city," he said. "Maybe someone
has seen our puppies."

So Pongo sent a message.
The message went from dog to dog.
"A howl, a growl, a yip, a yelp!
Dalmatian puppies need your help.
A bark, a woof, a long bow-wow!
Find our puppies. Find them now."

Soon all the dogs in the city were barking.

In an old barn near the city there lived
a horse named Captain, a dog named Colonel,
and a cat named Sergeant Tibbs.
That night they heard barking.
It was coming from the city.
"It's a message," said the Colonel.
"Someone is looking for Dalmatian puppies."
"None here, sir!" said Tibbs.

Then they heard more barking.
It was coming from a house down the road.
"Sounds like puppies!" said the Colonel.
"I believe you're right, sir!" said Tibbs.

"Then we must go and see if they are Dalmatian puppies," said the Colonel.

"Why do we have to do that?" asked the Captain.

"Because of the message," said Tibbs.

They marched down the road and up to
the old house.

The barking got louder and louder.

"How odd!" said the Colonel. "There
is a light in one window."

"Why is that so odd?" asked the Captain.

"Because no one lives here," said Tibbs.

They went to the window and peeked in.
The room was filled with Dalmatian puppies!
A man was holding a big, black bag.
It was filled with ten more Dalmatian puppies.

A woman in a fur coat was saying:

"Now I have ninety-nine Dalmatian puppies.
Tomorrow I will sell all of them to the circus
and the three of us will be rich!"

The three animals raced back to the barn.
Then the Colonel sent a message.
"Calling all dogs—every mutt and hound!
The Dalmatian puppies have been found.
A yip, a yelp, a short bow-wow!
Come and save them. Come right now."

Soon the city dogs
were barking again.

At last the **message** came to Pongo
and Perdy.

"The puppies **have** been found!" cried Pongo.
"We must go **and** save them."

And they **jumped** out the window.

Pongo and Perdy ran through the city.
The city dogs met them along the way.
They told Pongo and Perdy how to get
to the old barn.

When the Colonel saw them coming,
he called, "Are you looking for the
Dalmatian puppies?"

"Yes," they called back.

"Then follow us," said the Colonel.
"They are in an old house down the road."
So Pongo and Perdy followed the Colonel,
the Captain, and Sergeant Tibbs.

Pongo and Perdy went into the old house.

They saw two men with their puppies.

The two men saw them.

"Well, look who's here!" said Jasper.

"Two big ones! We'll take care of them,
won't we?"

Pongo growled and leaped at Jasper.

He bit into Jasper's jacket and pulled it
over Jasper's head.

Jasper could not see where he was going.

Next Tibbs leaped up into the air.
"MEOW!!!" screeched Tibbs.
He landed on Horace's head.
Horace was too scared to do anything.

Then Perdy pulled the rug right out
from under the two men.

Jasper and Horace crashed to the floor.

They were too surprised to move.

"That takes care of THEM," said Perdy.

"Now—where are our puppies?"

"Here we are!" called one puppy.

"All ninety-nine of us!"

"Ninety-nine puppies!" cried Pongo.

But there was no time to **ask** questions.

Pongo and Perdy led all **ninety**-nine puppies
out of the house.

They began to walk back to the city.
Suddenly they saw a woman in a car.
It was Cruella!
"Somebody stop those dogs!" she cried.
"I have to sell them to the circus."

When Pongo and Perdy heard this,
they hid the puppies in a shed.

Cruella looked all around.

"Now where did those little spotted
creeps go?" she said.

Pongo and Perdy were scared.

How could they get out?

"Look, Mom!" said one of the puppies.
She was rolling in a pile of soot.
"This is no time to play!" said Perdy.
"We have to think of a way to get out."
Then Perdy thought of a way to get out.
She told ALL the puppies to roll in the soot.

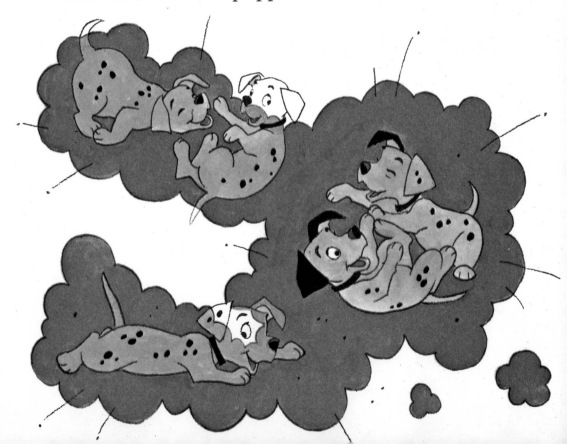

Soon they were all covered with soot.
Pongo and Perdy led the puppies outside.
They went right past Cruella.
Cruella paid no attention to them.
She was looking for white puppies with
black spots—not gray puppies!

They got into a truck
that was parked outside.

Just as the last puppy was getting in,
Cruella cried, "EEEK!"

Half of the puppy was gray.

But half of the puppy was white
with black spots.

Just then the truck drove away.

"STOP! STOP!" shouted Cruella.

"Come back with my puppies!"

But the truck driver did not hear her.

He was on his way to the city.

And that is how the Dalmatians got home

The two nice people who lived in the house
were happy to see them.
They were also a bit surprised.
Their family had grown.

Now there were Pongo and Perdy and ninety-nine puppies.

One hundred and one Dalmatians in all!

It was a good thing they were two very NICE people.